The Night Before
Kindergarten

Grosset & Dunlap
An Imprint of Penguin Group (USA) Inc.

For all the kindergarten teachers
who make school cool—NW

To my good friend Phoebe—JD

Text copyright © 2001 by Natasha Wing. Illustrations copyright © 2001 by Julie Durrell. Originally published in 2001 by Grosset & Dunlap. This edition published in 2013 as part of the *Night Before Kindergarten* gift set by Grosset & Dunlap, a division of Penguin Young Readers Group, 345 Hudson Street, New York, New York 10014. GROSSET & DUNLAP is a trademark of Penguin Group (USA) Inc. Manufactured in China.

Box Set ISBN 978-0-448-46784-9   10 9 8 7 6 5 4 3 2 1

The Night Before
Kindergarten

by Natasha Wing
illustrated by Julie Durrell

Grosset & Dunlap
An Imprint of Penguin Group (USA) Inc.

'Twas the night before kindergarten,
and as they prepared,
kids were excited
and a little bit scared.

They tossed and they turned
about in their beds,
while visions of school supplies
danced in their heads.

Erasers and crayons
and pencils galore
were stuffed in their backpacks
and set by the door.

Outfits were hung
in the closets with care,
knowing that kindergarten
soon would be there.

In the morning it came—
school starts today!
Would the teacher be nice?
Would they still get to play?

Faces were washed,
and teeth were brushed white;
kids posed for pictures
with eyes sparkling bright.

Parents packed snacks,
and kids hopped in cars
as if they were boarding
a spaceship to Mars.

Some kids brought blankets
or their favorite stuffed bear,
in hopes they could nap
like they did in day care.

Their parents exclaimed,
"You're big kids—wow!
Let us hold your bears
and blankies for now."

The parents were worried
their children would cry
if they left them at school
with just a good-bye.

So they told their darlings,
"If you want, we can stay
and make sure that everything
will be A-okay."

The teacher then greeted
each one with a smile,
and invited the students
to stay for a while.

The room was all filled
with toys, books, and maps,
but where were the beds
for midmorning naps?

They colored and painted
and played Simon Says,

then tumbled and skipped

and stood on their heads.

They sang silly songs
from beginning to end.
Within just a minute,
each kid had a friend.

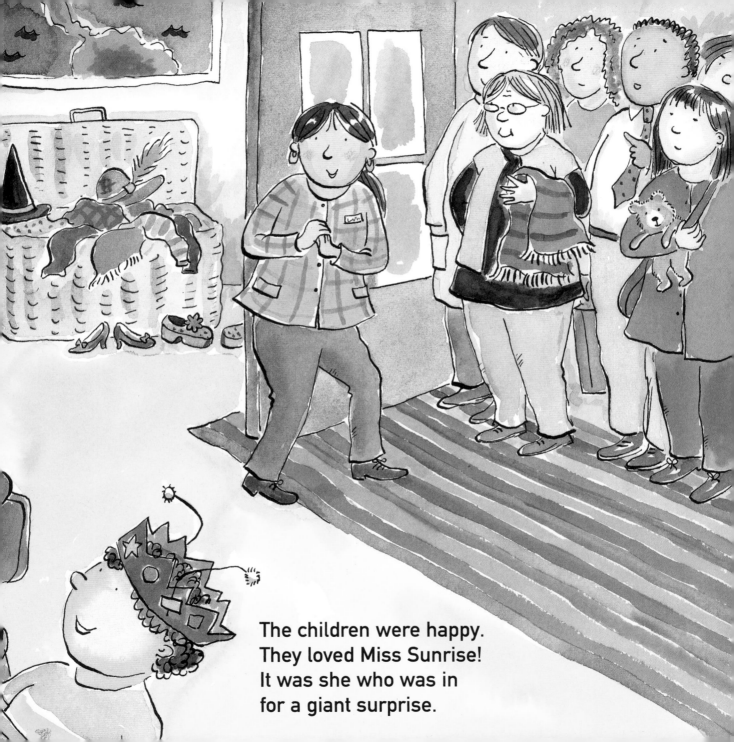

The children were happy.
They loved Miss Sunrise!
It was she who was in
for a giant surprise.

When what to her wondering eyes
should appear
but sad moms and dads
who were holding back tears!

Their noses—so sniffly!
Their eyes—red and wet!
This was the saddest good-bye
Miss Sunrise had seen yet!

She gathered the grown-ups
on the magical rug,
then sent them away
after one final hug.

The children all waved
from the door of the school.
"Don't cry, Mom and Dad;
kindergarten is cool!"